balancing

stretching

cooking

finding

measuring

bouncing

hiding

waiting

pulling

teaching

sliding

climbing

marching

throwing

tasting

standing

tickling

pointing

First published individually as
Bouncing and *Giving* (1993)
Hiding and *Chatting* (1994)

First U.S. edition in this form 1999

Library of Congress Cataloging-in-Publication Data

Hughes, Shirley.
Let's join in : four stories / Shirley Hughes.—1st U.S. ed.
p.   cm.
Summary: Hiding—Giving—Chatting—Bouncing.
ISBN 0-7636-0824-6
[1. Children's stories, English. 2. Play—Fiction. 3. Behavior—Fiction.
4. Short stories.]   I. Title.
PZ7.H8395Le   1999
[E]—dc21   98-21931

2 4 6 8 10 9 7 5 3 1

Printed in Italy

This book was typeset in Sabon.
The pictures were done in colored pencil, watercolor, and pen line.

Candlewick Press
2067 Massachusetts Avenue
Cambridge, Massachusetts 02140

Let's Join In

FOUR STORIES BY
Shirley Hughes

CANDLEWICK PRESS
CAMBRIDGE, MASSACHUSETTS

Contents

Hiding

You can't see me—I'm hiding!

Here I am.

I'm hiding again!
Bet you can't find me this time!

Under a bush in the yard is
a very good place to hide.
So is under a big umbrella,

or down at the
end of the bed.

Sometimes Dad hides
behind a newspaper,

and Mom hides
behind a book
on the sofa.

You can even hide
under a hat.

Tortoises hide inside their shells when they aren't feeling friendly,

and hamsters hide right at the back of their cages when they want to go to sleep.

When the baby hides his eyes, he thinks you can't see him. But he's there all the time!

A lot of things
seem to hide –
the moon behind
the clouds,

and the
sun behind
the trees.

Flowers need to hide in the
ground in the wintertime.

But they come peeping out
again in the spring.

Buster always hides when
it's time for his bath,

and so does Mom's wallet when
we're all ready to go shopping.

Our favorite place to hide is behind the kitchen door. Then we jump out—BOO!

And can you guess
who's hiding behind
these curtains?

You're right!—it's us!

Giving

I gave Mom a present on her birthday,
all wrapped up in pretty paper.
And she gave me a big kiss.

I gave Dad a very special picture which I
painted at play group. And he gave me a
ride on his shoulders most of the way home.

I gave the baby some slices
of my apple.

We ate them sitting under the table.

At dinnertime the baby gave me
two of his soggy bread crusts.

That wasn't much of a present!

You can give someone
an angry look . . .

or a big smile!

You can give a tea party . . .

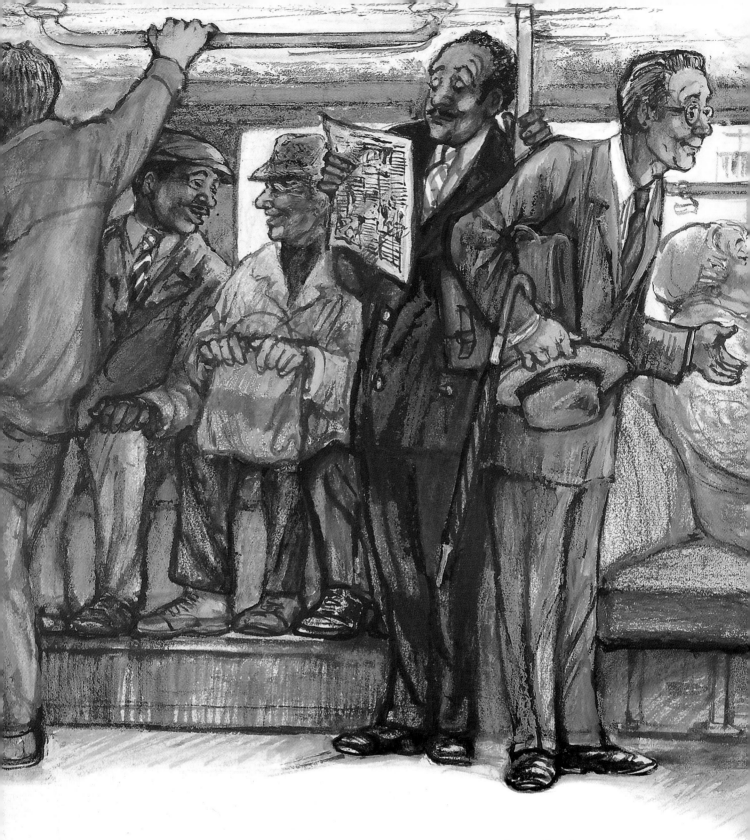

or a seat on a crowded bus.

On my birthday Grandma and Grandpa
gave me a beautiful doll carriage.
I said "Thank you," and gave
them each a big hug.

And I gave my dear Bemily
a ride in it, all the way
down the garden path
and back again.

I tried to give the cat a
ride too, but she gave me
a nasty scratch!

So Dad had to give
my poor arm a kiss and
a Band-Aid.

Sometimes, just when
I've built a big castle
out of blocks,

the baby comes along and
gives it a big swipe!
And it all falls down.

Then I feel like giving
the baby a big
swipe too.

But I don't, because he *is*
my baby brother, after all.

Chatting

I like chatting.

I chat to the cat,

and I chat
in the car.

I chat with
friends in
the park,

and with the lady at the
supermarket.

Grown ups like
chatting too.

Sometimes these
chats go on for
a very long time.

The lady next door is an
especially good chatter.

When Mom is busy, she says
that there are just too many
chatterboxes around.

So I go off and
chat to Bemily –
but she never
says a word.

The baby likes
to chat on his toy
telephone. He makes
a lot of calls.

But I can chat with
Grandma and Grandpa
on the real telephone.

Some of the best chats
of all are with Dad, when he
comes to say good night.

Bouncing

When I throw my big shiny ball . . .

it bounces away from me.

Bounce, bounce, bounce, bounce!

Then it rolls along the ground, and it stops.

I like bouncing too.

In the mornings I bounce on my bed,
and the baby bounces in his crib.

Mom and Dad's big bed is an
even better place to bounce.

But Dad doesn't like being
bounced on in the early morning.

So we roll on the floor instead, and
the baby bounces on ME!

After breakfast he
does some dancing
in his baby bouncer,

and I do some dancing
to the radio.

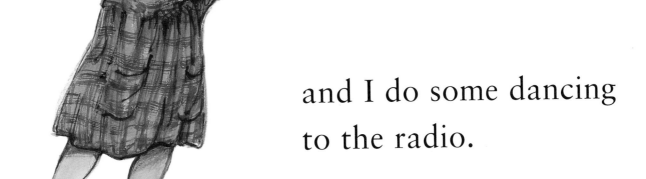

At my play group there are big cushions
on the floor where lots of children
can bounce together.

And at home there's
a big sofa where we
can bounce when
Mom isn't looking.

Grandpa and I know a good bouncing game.
I ride on his knees and we sing:

This is the way
the ladies ride:
trit-trot, trit-trot;

This is the way
the gentlemen ride:
giddy-up, giddy-up;

This is the way
the farmers ride:
clip-clop, clip-clop;

This is the way
the jockeys ride:
gallopy, gallopy...

and FALL OFF!

I like bouncing.

I bounce around all day . . .

bounce,
    bounce,
    bounce,
        bounce!

Until in the end I stop bouncing,
and go to sleep.

skipping   telling   listening   waving   dancing

shouting   eating   smelling   chatting   kicking

giving   stroking   thinking   crying   yawning

washing   sleeping   singing   writing   tearing